OUTBACK COUNTOUT

BY NORAH KERSH

Published by Boolarong Press, 1/655 Toohey Road, Salisbury, QLD, Australia 4107

© **Norah V Kersh 2001**

(07) 4741 8708

First Printed 2001

Reprinted 2004, 2006

National Library of Australia

Kersh, Norah

Outback Countout

ISBN: 0 8643 9210 9

To John, our children
and our on growing family
whose encouragement and inspiration
are always widening my horizons.

Acknowledgments

I would like to thank all those whose help has made this book possible, especially

Karen Redman, from Mount Isa School of the Air, for the valuable input, and advice.

Kerry McGinnis, of Bowthorn Station, whose writing has the power to bring tears to ones eyes.

My daughter Rosana for her ongoing help and patience, with layout and much more.

My sons, Brendan and Conor. Brendan with his flair for words has helped polish up mine, and

Conor for his generous promotion of my work.

Thank you John and all the rest of our lovely family for your interest and

encouragement which has helped me keep on track.

Also I would like to thank the readers of Outback Alphabet by whom I have been much encouraged.

I have been particularly touched by the people who have lived the life,

which in a small way I am aiming to depict.

Other books illustrated by the author:
"Outback Alphabet" Norah Kersh
"Through Deep Waters" Fran Spora
"Reflections from the Desert" Pat Cullen

Zero eggs in the nest as Zade takes a look, no eggs for breakfast. What a lazy chook!

One station homestead out on the plain,
one little boy wishing for some rain.

 **Two** working dogs balance on the bike,
jumping bumps, chasing sheep is their real delight

Three purple hills against the blue sky,
three children scatter, kites flying high.

Four fat bullocks along a dusty track,

followed by a pony, with Clancy on its back.

Five tall gum trees spread their friendly shade, underneath we picnic on billy-tea and lemonade.

Six patient horses standing here all day,
nodding heads and flicking tails, swish the flies away.

14

Seven hats awaiting to be worn in the sun,

Darcy waits on the verandah for his dad to come.

7

15

16

Eight little kids know that rodeos are fun,

cheer the riders, and the ropers,

and the bulls that weigh a tonne!

Nine woolly sheep jump as they go through the gate, stubborn old stragglers, for shearing they are late.

Ten sparkling stars set the sky alight,
now at the homestead, time to say "Goodnight".

A child believes without question, trusts without doubt, loves without fear

A child leaves yesterday behind, doesn't worry about tomorrow, lives for today

A child greets everyone, leaves doors open, knocks walls, laughs loudly, forgets

A child prays simply, cries heartily, forgives immediately.....

Peter Byrne CSSR

To Order this Book
Contact us at:

Boolarong
Press

1/655 Toohey Road, Salisbury, Queensland 4107

Phone: (07) 3373 7855   Fax: (07) 3373 8611

e-mail: mail@boolarongpress.com.au

Visit us online: www.boolarongpress.com.au